# Hello, Family Members,

Learning to read is one of the most important accomplishments of early childhood. **Hello Reader!** books are designed to help children become skilled readers who like to read. Beginning readers learn to read by remembering frequently used words like "the," "is," and "and"; by using phonics skills to decode new words; and by interpreting picture and text clues. These books provide both the stories children enjoy and the structure they need to read fluently and independently. Here are suggestions for helping your child *before, during,* and *after* reading:

## Before

- Look at the cover and pictures and have your child predict what the story is about.
- Read the story to your child.
- Encourage your child to chime in with familiar words and phrases.
- Echo read with your child by reading a line first and having your child read it after you do.

## During

- Have your child think about a word he or she does not recognize right away. Provide hints such as "Let's see if we know the sounds" and "Have we read other words like this one?"
- Encourage your child to use phonics skills to sound out new words.
- Provide the word for your child when more assistance is needed so that he or she does not struggle and the experience of reading with you is a positive one.
- Encourage your child to have fun by reading with a lot of expression . . . like an actor!

## After

- Have your child keep lists of interesting and favorite words.
- Encourage your child to read the books over and over again. Have him or her read to brothers, sisters, grandparents, and even teddy bears. Repeated readings develop confidence in young readers.
- Talk about the stories. Ask and answer questions. Share ideas about the funniest and most interesting characters and events in the stories.

I do hope that you and your child enjoy this book.

—Francie Alexander
   Reading Specialist,
   Scholastic's Learning Ventures

*For Brandi Roth*
*—C.B.*

Text copyright © 1999 by Cynthia Benjamin.
Illustrations copyright © 1999 by Jacqueline Rogers.
All rights reserved. Published by Scholastic Inc.
SCHOLASTIC, HELLO READER! and CARTWHEEL BOOKS and associated logos
are trademarks and/or registered trademarks of Scholastic Inc.

Library of Congress Cataloging-in-Publication Data

Benjamin, Cynthia.
    Footprints in the sand / by Cynthia Benjamin; illustrated by Jacqueline Rogers.
        p.  cm. — (Hello reader! Science. Level 1)
"Cartwheel books."
Summary: Pictures and simple text depict desert animals and the tracks they leave in the sand as they rush to their homes.
        ISBN 0-590-44087-X
        1. Desert animals—Juvenile fiction. [1. Desert animals—Fiction.
2. Animal tracks—Fiction. 3. Animals—Habitations—Fiction.] I. Rogers, Jacqueline, ill.
II. Title.  III. Series: Hello science reader! Level 1.
PZ10.3.B437F1 1999
[E]—dc21                                                                              98-11009
                                                                                          CIP
                                                                                          AC

10 9 8 7 6 5 4 3 2 1                                             9/9 0/0 01 02 03 04

Printed in the U.S.A.   24
First printing, May 1999

# Footprints in the Sand

by Cynthia Benjamin
Illustrated by Jacqueline Rogers

**Hello Reader! Science —Level 1**

SCHOLASTIC INC.

New York  Toronto  London  Auckland  Sydney

# Desert sun gleams.

# Desert sun glows.

# Someone races

home.

bobcat

# Someone flies
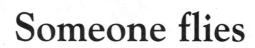

home.

gila woodpecker

Someone darts

home.

collared lizard

# Someone creeps

home.

tarantula

Someone crawls

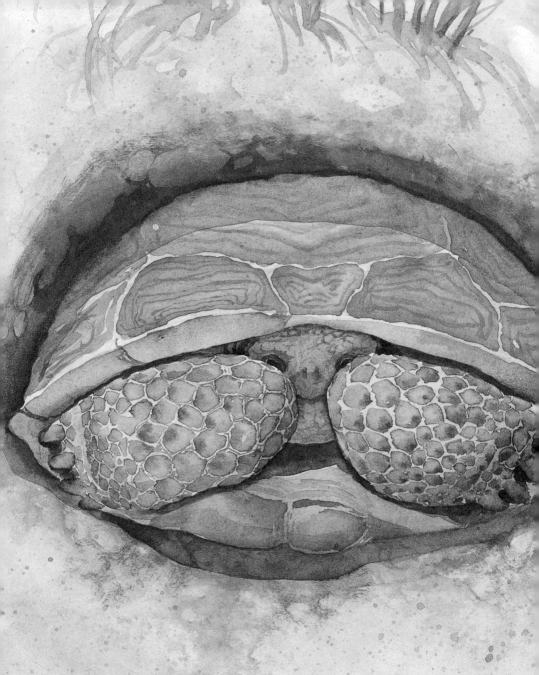

home.

desert tortoise

# Someone hops

home.

black-tailed jackrabbit

# Someone runs

home.

desert kit fox

Someone glides

home.

rattlesnake

Someone jumps

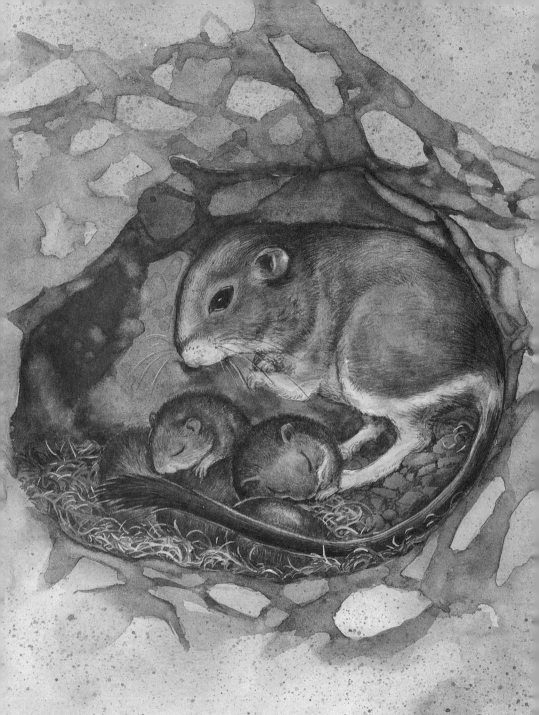

home.

kangaroo rat

Someone walks

home.

Desert sun gleams.
Desert sun glows.